Nine Tenners

Nine short plays
by
John Glass

"The Witch Makes Five"

"Raiders of the Lost Rakasa"

"It's Aunt Alice"

"Katie and the Crutches"

"Money in the Graveyard"

"A Day in Court"

"Mrs. Calapooza and the Culebra"

"Don't Let Bigfoot Bite!"

"The Great Galapanza"

john@studentplays.org

Copyright information. Please read!

☞ About Student Plays ☜

Student Plays consists of **John Glass, Jackie Jernigan,** and **Dominic Torres.** We are a group of playwrights and directors that have written scripts for elementary school through college. We are proud of the variety of ages that our scripts serve.

Student Plays has comedies, dramas, "creepy" plays, and also Latino-themed plays. These are scripts that focus on Latino youth and the Latino experience. Any school can perform a Latino-themed play: it just requires a general introduction and basic exposure to the Spanish language, something that most schools and students already have.

To contact *Student Plays* or to communicate with one of the playwrights, simply email us at john@studentplays.org.

4

Table of Contents

After a bizarre group camping trip, a student is checked into a youth mental facility. When she is visited by the other members of the trip, memories of the weekend trickle out . . . and horrific things begin to happen.

Seven young explorers arrive at a cave in a far-off land in search of the great "Rakasa." They find what they want . . . along with a few of the cave's unexpected surprises.

It's a pleasant evening at a local restaurant. That is, until Alice discovers that her two nieces are sitting at another table, avoiding her. What will Alice do??

Katie needs help! Due to an injury, she is on crutches, and desperately needs help with chores around the house. Or does she . . . ?

An old map leads a group of friends to a potential discovery in the local cemetery. But will the rumors of a "Pine Ghost" thwart their find?

☞ In each play, the names of the characters may be changed, giving flexibility to the gender of each character. *Any* gender can play *any* of the characters. ☜

The Witch Makes Five

The Witch Makes Five

<u>Characters of the Play</u>

JOYCE	High school student. Distraught. Agitated.
ROD	High school student. Nervous.
STACIE	High school student. Nervous.
WORKER 1	Either gender. Small role at the play's end.
WORKER 2	Either gender. Small role at the play's end.

The setting is a patient's room in a mental treatment center for the youth. JOYCE is a patient and is being visited by ROD and STACIE. She is wearing a hospital/facility gown or shirt. There are a few chairs, a small table with a telephone, and if possible, a bed or cot. Everyone is shaken and somewhat uncomfortable.

The time is the present, October, and there are several Halloween decorations hanging about. A witch face should be one of the decorations, prominently displayed.

This ten-minute spooky play is best suited for **middle school** or **high school.** The few allusions to "high school student" and so forth can easily be altered.

ROD and JOYCE are seated, in the middle of discussion.

ROD: Well, I'll tell you one thing.

JOYCE: What?

ROD: I'm never going camping again.

JOYCE: Man. No kidding!

ROD: And I'm also never going to go looking for *anything* in the middle of the woods. Stupid *StoneHouse* . . .

JOYCE: Well, let's be honest: something tells me the StoneHouse found *us*.

ROD: Tell me about it *(Beat.)* But you know what was really cool?

JOYCE: What?

ROD: Those wicked-looking pine trees! In the moonlight!

JOYCE: Don't start with the pine trees!

ROD: Seriously, Joyce. I wasn't going to mention it. But the way those needles silhouetted against the moon! Wow . . .

JOYCE: You are such a writer.

ROD: Come on, it was beautiful. We've got to find something positive out of all this. Right?

JOYCE: Um, I guess.

ROD: It was exotic.

JOYCE: Look. I don't want us to keep ignoring this. You know what we saw. Don't you?

ROD: Well . . . *(Uncomfortably)* I know what I *think* I saw.

JOYCE: You mean, you *know* what you saw.

ROD: Hmmph.

JOYCE: Come on, Stacie saw her too. Let's not pretend. Okay?

ROD: *(Quietly.)* Yeah. I know.

JOYCE: We all saw her. *(Beat. She is very distraught.)* But . . . Rod?

ROD: What?

JOYCE: You know what I absolutely *can't* pretend about that camping trip? I know we agreed to drop this for now. But Rod . . . there were four of us out there. *Four* of us!

ROD: Look, Joyce—

(Enter STACIE, carrying a small bottle/can of juice. She sets it down.)

JOYCE: *(Grabbing him by the arm.)* I know, I know. You guys think I lost it out in those woods. Both of you do!

ROD: I didn't say that!

STACIE: *(Groaning, at hearing the discussion)* Ughh!

JOYCE: But it was you, me, Stacie . . . and *Scottie*! Scottie was the one that organized the whole camping trip!

ROD: Joyce—

JOYCE: You guys have known him since that film class our freshman year! And I've known him for almost that long!

STACIE: Joyce? We know that you—

JOYCE: Oh, don't start, Stacie. I know what you're thinking! You've already said that I belong in here. That this place might be good for me for a little while.

STACIE: You know that I didn't mean it like that! Come on!

JOYCE: Whatever.

ROD: Joyce, it's just that we've already told you. We don't know a *Scottie!* We never have! It was you, Stacie and me! Three college idiots in the middle of the woods!

STACIE: Searching for something we never should have been looking for.

ROD: *(Slowly.)* Something . . *happened* out there, Joyce. Something really bizarre.

STACIE: Right.

ROD: Something that affected you.

JOYCE: Stacie, you believe that we saw something. Don't you?

(Pause. STACIE sits, and speaks slowly.)

STACIE: Oh, yeah. Absolutely. I told you that I did. That face . . . I can't get it out of my brain.

JOYCE: Okay. So if you remember that, don't you remember how Scottie walked right up to that window? Holding that flashlight?? Scottie was the first one to see her!!

STACIE: Joyce, that didn't happen! *Rod* was holding the flashlight! There *was* no Scottie! There were only *three* of us out there, Joyce.

JOYCE: There were FOUR OF US!! Us three, and *Scottie*!!
> (Pause.)
And that . . that *witch*. The witch makes five.
> (Off their look.)
Don't look at me like that!

ROD: Joyce, take your medication.

JOYCE: Ughhh.

STACIE: Yeah, here's the juice.

JOYCE: I don't have the pills yet. The nurse should be bringing them in a minute.

ROD: Okay. Well . . . relax. You're okay.

JOYCE: And anyway, I need water. The doctor said not to take medication with juice.

ROD: I'll go get some water.

STACIE: Sorry, I'll get it.

ROD: No, it's fine, I got it. There's a fountain down the hall.

JOYCE: There are cups in the nurse's office.

ROD: Be right back.

JOYCE: Thanks, Rod.

(Pause as he exits. JOYCE attempts to collect herself.)

JOYCE: I'm sorry, Stacie.

STACIE: It's okay. Just try and stay calm.

JOYCE: I know. I know.

STACIE: You'll be out of this place in no time.

JOYCE: I hope . . . *(Pause. She sighs, looks around the room.)* Damn. Do they have to have these stupid Halloween decorations in here?

STACIE: Well, it *is* October.

JOYCE: I know . . . but sheesh. I'm already freaked out as it is.
   (Beat. Still distraught.)
I apologize, Stacie. I'm just a wreck.

STACIE: It's fine.

JOYCE: No, I'm really a wreck. I'm eighteen years old and I had a nervous breakdown. What teenager does that?
   (Beat.)
And my parents, wow, they're all upset. I had to practically beg them to leave this afternoon, to get away for a few hours. To go grab some dinner.

STACIE: I talked to your teachers. They all know you'll be out of school for a bit.

JOYCE: Aggh! My classes!

STACIE: It's fine. They understood. You'll be out of here soon. Your teachers don't know *exactly* what you're going through but they know that it's serious.

JOYCE: Well, what we went through *was* serious.

STACIE: Gosh . . . don't remind me. It's . . . the *explaining* part that's eventually going to be tough. For *all* of us.

(*Pause as they reflect.*)

JOYCE: I can still see her. Her face. Uggh. Those wrinkled, bony hands, holding that candle. So vicious and dark.

STACIE: (*Slowly.*) Nobody knows, Joyce. Nobody.

JOYCE: What??

STACIE: I didn't tell anyone. About her.

JOYCE: Are you serious? No one??

STACIE: I mean . . . how can I? My parents don't know, or anyone else. I don't know if I'll ever tell a single person. (*Slowly.*) I just don't want to . . .

JOYCE: . . end up in here like I did?

STACIE: No. I didn't say that.

JOYCE: Well. You don't *have* to. It's all over your face.

STACIE: I'm sorry. I–

JOYCE: *(Holding a hand up.)* Don't. It's fine. I understand.

> *(Pause. They gather themselves, uncomfortably.)*

STACIE: Okay. Well. Yeah. Stupid StoneHouse.

JOYCE: I know . . .

STACIE: Stupid witch.

> *(Beat. JOYCE attempts to lighten things up.)*

JOYCE: And Rod! Ha! Rod screamed like a little girl!

> *(Pause as she laughs. STACIE stares at her in confusion.)*

STACIE: Who . . ?

JOYCE: *Rod,* Stacie. Our friend.

STACIE: Who the heck are you talking about?

JOYCE: ROD!! *(She jumps up and paces in anger.)* Oh, what is HAPPENING here?? First Scottie, and now Rod??

STACIE: Joyce—

JOYCE: He's our *friend*, Stacie! He's down the hall, getting water for my medication!

STACIE: Who are you talking about?? Nobody came to visit you but me!!

JOYCE: You came with Rod!! Our goofball writer friend!! *Rod,* Stacie! We went camping with him this weekend!!

STACIE: Joyce, I don't know a *Rod!* Or a *Scottie*! You and me went camping, and you and me *only*.

JOYCE: No!

STACIE: Joyce, get a grip of yourself!

JOYCE: I've *got* a grip of myself! It's everybody else I'm worried about!! *(Tears down the witch decoration.)* I should have taken that down a long time ago!

STACIE: Look, I'm going to call one of the nurses. *(Moves to pick up the phone.)*

JOYCE: *(Calling down the hallway.)* ROD?? Rod, get in here! Rod!!

STACIE: *(On phone)* Hello . .? Hello! I need help in Room 8!

JOYCE: ROD!

(She exits, calling his name.)

STACIE: Joyce, come back! *(Back on phone.)* Hello? Is anyone there?? Hello??
    (Pause.)
Oh, yes, I am in room 8, and I really need your help! The patient here just ran out!
    (Pause.)
What?? What do you mean, *there's no patient in this room*?? Joyce Carol is in this room! Room 8!
    (Pause. She repeats herself.)
Her name is Joyce Carol! I'm here visiting her! Hello? Did you hear me?? HELLO??
    (Slams the phone down. She turns to the hall way, and begins to exit.)
JOYCE?? JOYCE!!

(She runs out, calling her name. Long pause. Enter two workers from the _other_ side of the stage. They are carrying a broom, cleaning materials, and a clipboard with papers.)

WORKER ONE: You brought the dustpan, didn't you?

WORKER TWO: Yep. Right here.

WORKER ONE: Okay. Nobody's been in here for a few days so it's probably a little dusty.

WORKER TWO: Can't believe how quiet it's been all day.

WORKER ONE: I know. It's like a ghost town.

WORKER TWO: I wish it were always this quiet.
 (Pause.)
How many do we have left to clean?

WORKER ONE: Two more. But they want this room ready by the morning, for a new patient.

WORKER TWO: Yeah.

WORKER ONE: *(Picking up the witch decoration.)* Looks like one of the decorations fell off the wall.

WORKER TWO: Ugghh. I've never liked witches.

WORKER ONE: Ha. I've always liked them. This needs to go back on the wall.

WORKER TWO: Mmmm. If you say so . . .

(They continue working in silence. Lights fade. End of play.)

Raiders of the Lost Rakasa

Raiders of the Lost Rakasa

<u>Characters</u>

HUNTER	Male. Adventurer. Leader of the group.
CHRISTINE	Female. Adventurer.
MILTON	Male. Adventurer.
JENNY	Female. Adventurer.
LAMONICA	Female. Easily scared.
JOHN	Male. Easily scared.
SALLY	Female. Easily scared.

The time is the present, the setting a large cave, somewhere far away. On the far side of the stage should be a simple pedestal or small altar, perhaps two or three feet high, with the "Rakasa" on top. The Rakasa is simply a book, wrapped in gold or silver paper; it, however, should *look* like a sacred idol.

Once it is wrapped, the shape should not resemble a book.

On the other side of the stage is an entry-way into the "cave." The entry-way can be an easy arrangement of aluminum/plastic or pvc-tubing, four to five feet wide, draped in cobwebs or old torn sheets.

All of the characters are dressed in adventurer/explorer clothing, such as safari khakis, boots, straw fedoras, satchels, etc. CHRISTINE should have a small bag of sand.

An assortment of toy rubber snakes are needed for this play.

The group is just outside the entry to the cave, about to enter.

HUNTER: Okay. This is it! The entrance to the great Rakasa!

LAMONICA: Yeah! This is where the other guys cashed in.

JOHN: Huh? Who?

MILTON: You know, the other guys. The great explorers.

CHRISTINE: Pierre Pancake! José Javalina! Lana the Lasso!

SALLY: Oh yeah. Those dudes. But are we *all* going to go in there?

HUNTER: Of course. Come on.

LAMONICA: Uh . . . I'll stay here.

MILTON: What? Are you serious?

LAMONICA: Yep. I'll stand guard.

JENNY: Why??

LAMONICA: You know. In case someone comes.

JOHN: Me too.

CHRISTINE: You guys are scared!

SALLY: Yep. Hey, guilty as charged. I *know* I'm scared. I'm staying here too.

HUNTER: But come on! This is the Rakasa we're talking about!

SALLY: I don't care if it's all the lemon pie on the planet. It looks creepy in there.

JOHN: Very creepy!

LAMONICA: Yep.

MILTON: Okay. Whatever. *(To the others.)* You guys ready?

HUNTER: Yes!

JENNY: Let's do this. Come on!

HUNTER: Okay . . . here we go.

LAMONICA: I'll say a prayer!

JOHN: I'll say two!

SALLY: I'll say three!

CHRISTINE: Oh, hush!!

(They enter the cave slowly. LAMONICA, JOHN, and SALLY all quietly exit.)

JENNY: Wow. It's dark.

MILTON: No kidding.

HUNTER: Okay . . . go slow. Easy.

CHRISTINE: I can't believe I traveled 4000 miles for *this.*

MILTON: I know. Mosquito bites. Mud and sweat!

JENNY: No hot baths. No television!

CHRISTINE: No "Desperate Housewives"!

HUNTER: Stop! Come on, look. *(Pointing ahead.)* Do you guys see it?

CHRISTINE: Yep. Is that it?

HUNTER: That's it! The great Rasaka! Come on. Be careful where you walk. Don't step in the red areas.

JENNY: Why not?

HUNTER: Because if you do, poison darts will fly out of the walls!

MILTON: What??

HUNTER: Come on, didn't you see the movie??

CHRISTINE: Oh, yeah! The poison darts.

HUNTER: Come on, keep moving.

JENNY: This is not what I bargained for!!

MILTON: No kidding!
     (Beat. He notices something on the floor.)
Wait . . . what is that?

JENNY: It's . . . oh no.

MILTON: It's . . .

HUNTER: *(With great anguish.)* Snakes. Why did it have to be snakes??

CHRISTINE: Ohh!!

MILTON: Uggh!

HUNTER: Wisconsin vipers. Very dangerous.

JENNY: Go around them!

(They begin to do so.)

MILTON: That one is huge!!

HUNTER: Careful!

CHRISTINE: Ugghhh!

HUNTER: Okay . . . boy, those things are ugly.

MILTON: Yes they are!

JENNY: *(Focusing on the Rakasa.)* Look: there it is! The great Rakasa!

HUNTER: Okay, we have to grab it carefully . . . do you have that bag, Christine?

CHRISTINE: *(Hands him the bag of sand)* Yep. Right here.

HUNTER: Okay. Wow . . . here we go.

MILTON: Yes! We are finally doing this!

JENNY: I know!

HUNTER: *(Preparing to swap the Rakasa with the bag of sand)* Okay . . . one . . two . . three . .

> *(Pause as he swaps the two. Everybody breathes a sigh of relief.)*

CHRISTINE: That's it!

MILTON: Yeah! You did it!

JENNY: I can't believe it was that easy!

HUNTER: I know! Wow!

> *(A low rumbling noise is suddenly heard. The sound quickly becomes louder.)*

HUNTER: Wait . . maybe it *wasn't* that easy!

CHRISTINE: What is that noise? What's happening?

JENNY: The temple is coming down!

MILTON: No!!

HUNTER: Go! Run!

CHRISTINE: Aghh!

(They all run back to the entrance, screaming, dodging the snakes, diving and tumbling through the entry to the cave. LAMONICA, JOHN, and SALLY run over to meet them.)

MILTON: Agghhhh!!!

CHRISTINE: Ohhh!!

HUNTER: Boy, they don't come any closer than that.

JENNY: Amen to that!!

JOHN: Guys! What happened??

JENNY: The temple came crashing down!

MILTON: Yeah, it was epic!

SALLY: You guys got the Rakasa?

HUNTER: Yep. Right here.

SALLY: Sweet!

LAMONICA: Wow, there it is.

JOHN: Man! The Rakasa!

(HUNTER begins to remove the paper/ wrapping.)

SALLY: What are you doing?

HUNTER: I'm opening it! What do you think I'm do-ing??

JENNY: That, uh, comes off . . ?

HUNTER: Yep.

LAMONICA: Whaa . . ?

JOHN: Okay, this does *not* look good.

MILTON: What is that? It's . . . *español*?

JENNY: Huh?

SALLY: A Spanish book?

HUNTER: Si! The great Rakasa! Aquí está! A Spanish book! Mira . . .
(Opening it, reading the inside.)
"Ándele. Buenas tardes. Por favor!!"

CHRISTINE: We came 4000 miles for *this*?

MILTON: A Spanish book?

HUNTER: Not *just* a Spanish book! The Rakasa!!

JOHN: I can't believe this!

SALLY: Does anybody else want to strangle him besides me??

LAMONICA: *(Suddenly sees something in the distance.)* Guys, look!

CHRISTINE: What?

JOHN: *(Also looking off in the distance.)* Who is that?

HUNTER: The Indians!

JENNY: Who??

HUNTER: The Indians!! This is the part where they chase us!!

LAMONICA: Oh yeah! Come on, let's get out of here! Back to the plane!

HUNTER: Run!

> *(Everyone except for JOHN begins to flee in the same direction.)*

JENNY & **SALLY:** Agghhh!!

CHRISTINE: Go! Go!

MILTON: To the airplane!

JOHN: Guys?? Wait!!

(They all stop and turn to face JOHN.)

CHRISTINE: What?

SALLY: What is it??

HUNTER: Come on!! Hurry!

JOHN: *(Pointing in the other direction.)* The plane is THAT WAY!!

ALL except for JOHN: AGGHHH!!

(They begin to run in the other direction, stumbling and screaming. End of play.)

It's Aunt Alice!

It's Aunt Alice!
Characters

ZOE   Customer at restaurant.

REESE   Customer at restaurant. Sister of ZOE.

ALLIE   Neighbor of Aunt Alice.

ALICE   Grouchy. Complainer.

LYDIA   Waitress.

The time is the present, the setting a local restaurant.

Needs: menus, a serving tray and other typical items used by a waiter, several tables and chairs, a few large fake plants.

** The role of Alice should fit the classic caricature of an "old woman," best played by a student with a wig, pearls, an outdated dress, and a purse. **

ZOE and REESE are seated in Gambini's, a restaurant, and have just ordered. After a brief moment, ALICE and ALLIE enter with the waiter, and the waiter sits them.

ZOE Boy, this is nice!

REESE I know! Gambini's! So nice!

ZOE We are finally eating here.

REESE I'm eating *all* of my pasta fantastica!

    (Enter LYDIA, ALLIE and ALICE.)

ZOE I'm going to *destroy* my pasta magnifica!

REESE Pasta, pasta! I can't wait!

LYDIA Right this way.

ALLIE Oh, thank you.

LYDIA Is this table okay? Right here?

ALICE Yes. I guess so.

ZOE *(Seeing Alice.)* Oh no.

REESE Oh no, *what*? *(Sees ALICE.)* Oh.

ALLIE This is so nice.

ZOE Is that . . ?

REESE It can't be!

ZOE It's . . .

REESE It's . .

ZOE It's Aunt Alice!!

LYDIA Would you like some water?

ALLIE Please . . .

ALICE Yes, please.

LYDIA I'll be right back!

ALICE And waiter? Excuse me . . .

LYDIA Yes?

ALICE Hurry it up. I'm thirsty.

LYDIA Um, okay.

ALLIE Alice!

　　　　(She exits.)

ZOE What is she doing here??

REESE Aghh, she is such a pain!

ZOE Ughhhhh!!!

ALICE I am hungry!!

ZOE Big surprise. She's *always* hungry.

REESE I know.

ALICE And it sure is hot in here!

(*She stands and pulls off coat, puts it on her chair. ZOE and REESE duck behind their menus.*)

ZOE Quick! Hide! I don't want her to see us!

REESE I know, she's probably mad at us.

ZOE We missed her birthday party.

REESE Uh, you mean, her last *two* birthday parties.

ZOE Oh, right!

ALICE This place is a dump!

ALLIE Alice! Be nice!

ALICE Well, it is. Gambini's. More like *Slambini's!*

ALLIE Come on. What are we going to order?

ALICE I don't know . . .

(ZOE and REESE slowly lower their menus.)

ZOE She can't see us. Remember: she's blind!

REESE She is *not* blind!

ZOE Might as well be. Anyway, it's crowded in here. She won't see us.

REESE What do we do?

ZOE I don't know! We have to get outta here! If she sees us, she'll be mad for missing her birthday party.

(Enter LYDIA, carrying the water and food. She serves water to Alice's table first.)

REESE Aghh, she drives me bananas.

ZOE No kidding. I don't want to talk to her!

LYDIA Okay . . . here we go. Two waters.

ALLIE Thank you

ALICE Um . . . is the water clean?

LYDIA What?

ALICE Is the water clean??

LYDIA Of course!

ALICE Are you sure?

ALLIE Alice!! Goodness!

LYDIA Yes, it's clean.

ALICE I'm only asking!

LYDIA I'll be right back to get your order.

ALLIE Thank you.

(LYDIA walks over to serve the others their food.)

ALLIE Alice, I can't believe you!

ALICE What? I like clean water! What's the big deal??

ALLIE Ohhhh!!! It's always something with you!

LYDIA Okay . . . here we go . . . la pasta fantástica.

ZOE Mmmmm.

LYDIA La pasta magnífica.

REESE Mmmmm.

LYDIA And some nice warm bread.

ZOE & **REESE** Mmmmmm.

ZOE Looks good! Thank you!

LYDIA I'll be right back!

(*She walks away. They look at their food in sadness.*)

ZOE What a pity! We can't even eat our food!

REESE (*Trying to eat a small bite.*) Maybe just a little bit . . .?

ZOE No, not even a little bit. We've got to get outta here!

REESE Awwww!

ZOE (*Pulling out money.*) Here . . . here's the money. This should cover the bill.

REESE What a waste! That was babysitting money!

ZOE I know . . . but oh well . . . I don't want aunt Alice to see us.

REESE Adiós, pasta!

ZOE Okay, I'm going first.

REESE How?

ZOE I'll hide behind those plants. *(Pointing.)*
Right over there.

REESE Uh . . . okay.

> *(Enter LYDIA, ready to take the other
> table's order.)*

ZOE She's blind, she'll never see me. I'll go first. And
then, you go. Then we'll sneak outta here!

REESE Okay . . . sounds good!

> *(ZOE sneaks over behind the first plant.)*

LYDIA Okay . . . are we ready?

ALLIE Yep. All set.

LYDIA For you?

ALLIE I'll have the pasta magnífica.

LYDIA Excellent. And for you?

ALICE Um . . I'd like fried lobster.

ALLIE Huh??

LYDIA What?? Fried lobster?

ALICE Yes.

LYDIA Oh. Well, we don't have that here.

ALICE Why not?

LYDIA Why *not*? We just don't. This is Gambini's. We have Italian food.

ALICE What kind of place doesn't have fried lobster??

ALLIE Alice! Be respectful.

ALICE Well, it's true! *(Beat. She is distracted by Zoe's movement, behind the plant.)* Hey . . . what . . . what was that?

ALLIE Alice! Would you order??

ALICE I thought I saw something! Sorry!

ALLIE Come on!

ALICE Okay, I'll have the pasta fantasti-whatever . .

LYDIA La pasta fantastica.

ALICE That. Yes. I'll have that.

LYDIA Okay.

ALICE *(To the waiter.)* So . . . can you *go* please?

ALLIE Alice, you are unbelievable!

> *(REESE sneaks over behind the plant. ZOE sneaks away and exits.)*

ALICE What? She has to go and get our food, right?

ALLIE Ughhhhhh!

LYDIA It's okay, I'm going. *(Turns and exits.)*

ALLIE Good grief. I can't take you anywhere!

ALICE Oh, relax. It's fine. No big deal. *(Beat. She now sees REESE, hiding.)* Wait . . . um . . . Reese?? Is that you??

REESE Oh . . . hey! Aunt Alice!

ALLIE Who's that?

ALICE It's my niece, Reese. What are you doing here?

REESE Oh, just hanging out. You know!

ALICE You are . . . ?

REESE Sure! Um. I work here!

ALICE Uh . . . okay.

REESE And I have work to do! Gotta go!

ALICE Wait a minute. Hang on. Were you just . . . having dinner here?

REESE What?

ALICE And were you just trying to sneak away?

REESE No!

ALICE I think you were! You don't work here!

REESE I was just . . just . .

ALICE And why did you miss my birthday party??
(Standing up, grabbing purse.)

ALLIE Um, you told me it was your last *three* birth-day parties.

(Enter LYDIA, holding a platter.)

ALICE Right! It *was* three!

REESE But aunt Alice . . !

ALICE Don't you aunt-Alice me! *(Swings her purse at her.)* This will teach you a lesson!

(REESE ducks down and the purse hits LYDI A'S tray. Food goes everywhere.)

LYDIA Ohhh!!

REESE Look what you did!

LYDIA Oh my goodness!

ALLIE Alice! I can't believe you!!

ALICE I can't believe that I missed *her*. Come here, young lady! *(Begins to chase her.)* Wait until I tell your mother!

REESE Aghhh!

ALICE I am calling your mama tonight! I'll teach you to not ignore me at a restaurant!

REESE Aunt Alice, no!

ALICE Don't you aunt-Alice me!!

REESE No!!

ALICE Come here, young lady!

REESE Help!!

(They exit in a mad scramble. Long pause. LYDIA and ALLIE look at each other.)

ALLIE Oh gosh! I am so sorry! I can't believe her!

LYDIA Well . . . it's fine. It's okay.

ALLIE Look at this mess!

LYDIA It's fine . . . I can clean it up later.

ALLIE Ohhh!

LYDIA It's time for my break, anyway.

ALLIE Really?

LYDIA Yes. And look . . .*(Pointing to the other table)* . . . *their* food is still here.

ALLIE Uh . . . yes. It actually is! *(Pause as she looks at the food.)* I am hungry. Um. Are you?

LYDIA Me? I'm very hungry!

ALLIE *(Pointing to table.)* Shall we?

LYDIA Why not?

>	*(They shake hands as they walk over to the table.)*

ALLIE My name is Allie.

LYDIA My name is Lydia. I'm sorry that your friend left you by yourself.

ALLIE Well, it's okay. And you know what?

LYDIA What?

ALLIE She drives me crazy anyway.
    (Pause.)
She's *Aunt Alice!*

LYDIA Ha. Right!

    (They raise their glasses in a toast.)

ALLIE Ahhhh . . . bon appetit? *(Clink.)*

LYDIA Bon appetit!

    (End of play.)

Katie and the Crutches

Katie and the Crutches

KATIE   Bossy. Throughout the play, Katie is faking an injury.

STEVE   Exhausted from working.

KRYSTA   Exhausted from working.

LILY   Exhausted from working.

ALAINA   Exhausted from working.

The time is the present, the setting is the living room in Katie's house. The characters are all friends.

Needs: one pair of crutches, several brooms and dustpans, a duster, other typical household cleaning tools, a food tray with various food items.

As the lights go up, KATIE is on her crutches, standing, in pain from a leg injury. She is on the phone with her Aunt Charlotte. STEVE and LILY are doing various chores in the room, sweeping, cleaning, etc.

KATIE: No, it's fine, aunt Charlotte.
   (Pause.)
Yes! I'll be fine. I have my friends here to help me.
   (Pause.)
Yes. I know!!
   (Pause.)
Okay, thanks. I will. Bye, aunt Charlotte. Thank you. And don't you worry about a thing!! My friends are here! Bye!

   (She hangs up. Pause as she winces in pain.)

STEVE: What did she say?

KATIE: I told her not to come over.

LILY: Why?

KATIE: Because you guys are here, helping me. Besides, my aunt is busy.

STEVE: Well . . . what about your parents?

KATIE: I talked to them earlier. They're coming home Wednesday night.

LILY: Wednesday . . . ?

STEVE: *Night . . . ?*

KATIE: Yes. They couldn't get an earlier flight back from Chicago.

LILY: Wow. That's two days away.

KATIE: I know . . . *(In pain.)* Ohhh!! *(She sits down.)*

STEVE: Your leg still hurts, huh?

KATIE: Yes! Of course!

STEVE: Well, what did the doctor say? You never told us.

KATIE: He said I'll need these crutches for three weeks!

LILY: Three weeks?

STEVE: That's a long time. Katie, we feel so bad about this.

KATIE: Well, you should! I told you I didn't want to play that dumb wrestling game!

LILY: It was an accident.

STEVE: Yeah.

KATIE: I still told you guys. *(Wincing.)* Ohhh!!

LILY: Well . . . are you going to need any more help around the house?

KATIE: Absolutely!

LILY: Absolutely . . ?

KATIE: Yes. There's a lot to do. It's my parents' anniversary. And I need everything to be clean when they get home.

STEVE: Uh . . . everything?

KATIE: Yep. There's lots to do. The kitchen. The bathroom.

LILY: The *bathroom?*

KATIE: Yep. It's only fair, right? You guys forced me into that game . . . and I got hurt . . . right?

LILY: Um. Right.

STEVE: Right. Sort of.

KATIE: And also, I need your help. I can't make my lunch! My dinner!

LILY: But we've been here all morning! Working!

KATIE: Well, it's okay. I have Krysta and Alaina here to help me too. For now.

STEVE: *(Relieved.)* Yes you do!

KATIE: But I will still need you guys later on today.

LILY: Later on . . ?

STEVE: *Today . . ?*

KATIE: Yep. And tomorrow too.

STEVE: What?? Tomorrow?

> *(Enter KRYSTA and ALAINA, carrying food on a tray. They are tired from working.)*

KATIE: Yes. My parents don't get back until Wednesday night. So there's work to be done. And I obviously can't do it!

KRYSTA: Here we go . . . lunchtime.

KATIE: Ahh, perfect! Did you make soup?

ALAINA: Yes.

KATIE: With bread?

KRYSTA: Yes . . .

KATIE: Crackers?

ALAINA: Yes. We have everything.

KATIE: Excellent. You can put it right there on the table.

LILY: Okay, is there anything else, Katie?

STEVE: Yeah, we're tired! We're ready to go!

KATIE: I think you guys can go. Alaina and Krysta are here so they can help me.

KRYSTA: Huh?

ALAINA: Still . . ?

KATIE: Yep. *(Pointing to LILY and STEVE.)* And you two can go. But come back later!

> *(STEVE and LILY hurriedly and eagerly begin to exit.)*

STEVE: Okay. Have fun, you guys.

LILY: Yeah!

STEVE: Adiós!!

ALAINA: Later.

KATIE: See you guys in a few hours.

(They exit in a hurry. KATE begins to stir the soup.)

KATIE: Ahhh. This is nice. But, ohh . . . my leg.

ALAINA: Again?? More pain?

KATIE: Yes. Could you please put that pillow under my foot?

KRYSTA: Yes. *(Grabs a pillow and does so.)*

KATIE: That would be nice. Thanks.

KRYSTA: Here you go.

KATIE: Careful!

KRYSTA: I am!

KATIE: *(Helping her arrange the pillow.)* Okay, right there. Much better.
        (Beat.)
Now . . . I need one of you to sweep the back patio.

KRYSTA: What??

KATIE: The patio. You know. I want it to be clean when my parents arrive.

ALAINA: The patio is full of leaves! Thousands of them!

KATIE: Exactly! And it's obvious that I can't do it . . . right?

KRYSTA: Well . . .

KATIE: Right?

ALAINA: Right. I guess so . . .

KATIE: Good. So, the broom is already on the patio. Alaina, you can begin now. Krysta can bag them up when you're done.

ALAINA: *(Grudgingly begins to exit.)* Oh. Okay.

KATIE: Chop-chop!

ALAINA: I'm going!! I'm going!!

> *(She exits quickly.)*

KATIE: Good. Okay, that's taken care of. Now . . . where was I?

KRYSTA: You were about to eat your soup.

KATIE: Right! My soup. Okay, here we go . . .
(She begins to eat her soup. KRYSTA tries to exit, slowly.)

KATIE: Mmmmm. Boy, this is good. Really, really good. *(Beat. Sees KRYSTA leaving.)* Um, excuse me?? Are you leaving?

KRYSTA: Ummm, yes! I just wanted to get a snack for myself.

KATIE: Well, I could use some juice.

KRYSTA: Juice?

KATIE: Yes. Please?

KRYSTA: Oh, okay.

KATIE: Thanks. And there are some cookies in the kitchen. Bring those.

KRYSTA: Cookies?? And juice??

KATIE: I'm hungry! And I'm in pain!

KRYSTA: Sorry! Okay!

KATIE: The doctor said food will distract the pain! I have to obey his orders!

KRYSTA: *(Exiting.)* I'm going, I'm going!

KATIE: Thank you! And don't forget that you have to help Alaina after you bring me that.

KRYSTA: Good grief! I know!

> *(KRYSTA exits. After a moment, KATIE looks around, then tosses the crutches to the side. She stands and begins to walk around freely, doing a jig as she speaks.)*

KATIE: Ahhh! Life is pretty good. My lunch is made! My dinner will be made! The patio is being swept. The house is being cleaned. Ha! I'll have to get hurt more often!

> *(Pause. She sits back down, sips more of her soup, then sits back and relaxes, closing her eyes)*

Yes. I'll have to get hurt more often. I really will!

> *(Long pause. Her eyes remain closed and the lights fade to black. Here, to indicate a quick scene break, there can be a simple music cue. After a few seconds, the lights quickly come back up. KATIE is still seated, now napping. Enter STEVE, LILY, and KRYSTA. They are weary from all of the work. KATIE hears them and sits up abruptly. She is very animated here, exaggerating her appreciation.)*

KATIE: Well . . . hello!

STEVE: We finished the work. It took forever!

KATIE: Wow. All of it?

LILY: Yes. The bedrooms.

KATIE: Super!

KRYSTA: The bathroom.

KATIE: Spectacular!

STEVE: The dining room.

KATIE: *(Singing.)* "The dining room, the—"

LILY: Will you stop??

KATIE: What?? What did I do??

LILY: We are exhausted, Katie. We're your friends. But we've done a lot of work!

KRYSTA: Tell me about it!

> *(Enter ALAINA, exhausted, holding a plate with a piece of cherry pie.)*

STEVE: Vacuuming, sweeping, scrubbing! Your bedroom was disgusting!

KRYSTA: Yes. It. Was.

KATIE: Well, I *am* hurt, you know.

ALAINA: And *I* am hungry.

KATIE: Excuse me?

ALAINA: I'm going to sit down right here and eat this.

KATIE: Is that my cherry pie?

KRYSTA: Uh, your last piece of cherry pie.

KATIE: What??

LILY: I ate the second-to-last piece!

ALAINA: Sorry but this girl needs food. I swept the whole patio. And I raked the yard.

KATIE: I was going to eat that!

ALAINA: Oh well. I'm hungry!

> *(She raises her fork to eat when KATIE jumps up and runs over, grabs the plate from her.)*

KATIE: Stop! I told you! That is *my* pie!

ALAINA: Ohhhh!

KATIE: Not *yours!!*

> *(Pause. Everybody stares at her and gasps, in total shock.)*

ALAINA: Uhhh . . .

STEVE: What??

KRYSTA: You . . . can walk?

KATIE: Ohh!! Well, hallelulah! That medicine sure did work!

ALAINA: I can't believe it!

KATIE: Neither can I! What a miracle!

LILY: Katie, cut the comedy!

STEVE: Yeah! You were lying to us!

KATIE: No!

KRYSTA: How could you . . . ?

ALAINA: *(With disdain.)* I don't even know you any-more!

LILY: Neither do I!

KATIE: *(Drops to her knees)* Oh, guys, please, please, please forgive me!

STEVE: Why should we?

KATIE: I just found out my leg was okay!

LILY: What?

KATIE: Seriously! The doctor called and told me! While you guys were outside working!!

LILY: But were you going to tell us??

KATIE: Yes!

KRYSTA: Are you sure?

KATIE: Yes!

ALAINA: But you just said that you were still hurt! You weren't going to tell us!

(They all advance towards her.)

LILY: Tell the truth, woman! You didn't get hurt in that wrestling game!

STEVE: Yeah! You made us do all that work!

KATIE: No, wait!!

LILY: Let's get her!

KRYSTA: Hold her down!

KATIE: Guys, WAIT!!

    (They come to a stop. Pause.)

KATIE: Look, I'm sorry that I lied to you. I'll make it up to you. I promise!

ALAINA: How?

KATIE: I'm come and clean your bedrooms.

LILY: Really?

KATIE: And your bathrooms.

STEVE: Really?

KATIE: And your kitchens!

KRYSTA: Really?

ALAINA: What about the leaves in our yards?

KATIE: I'll rake them!

LILY: I've got a big backyard.

STEVE: And I've got a messy bedroom.

KATIE: I'll do it. All of it!

STEVE: When??

KATIE: I'll get started right now! Come on let's go!

(They begin to exit.)

LILY: Okay . . . but my house is first!

ALAINA: No, *my* house is first!

STEVE: No, *my* house is first!

(In their haste KATIE falls down.)

KRYSTA: Be careful!

KATIE: Aghh! Oh!

ALAINA: Oh no.

KATIE: Oh, my leg!

LILY: Are you okay?

KATIE: *(In great pain.)* Ohhh!!!

STEVE: I can't believe this!

KRYSTA: Neither can I!!

KATIE: Guys . . . ?

LILY: What??

ALAINA: Don't tell me . . .

KRYSTA: Please don't tell me . . !

KATIE: My leg really is hurt!!!

> *(Everybody except for KATIE turns to the audience at the same time.)*

STEVE, LILY, ALAINA & KRYSTA: NOT AGAIN!!

> *(They all turn back to her, groaning and staring. Lights fade to black. End of play.)*

Money in the Graveyard

Money in the Graveyard

MOLLY   Not scared of woods. Wants
to find money!

GARY   Not scared of woods. Wants
to find money!

BOBBY   Prankster.

LEXI   Prankster.

McKENNA   Very scared of the woods.

AVA   Adventurous.

EMMA   Adventurous.

MIGUEL   Very scared of the woods.

The time is the present, the setting a school and a nearby graveyard.

Scene One takes place at a school. **Scene Two** takes place in the graveyard. **Scene Three** takes place back at the school.

Needs: flashlights, pine straw, tree branches, grave-stones (optional), a large bag of counterfeit money, small shovels/spades, old books, a yellowed map and backpacks.

MOLLY and GARY are just joining BOBBY and LEXI, who are looking over several old books. The students are all at school, about to go to class.

MOLLY: Okay, so tell us. What did you guys want to show us?

GARY: Yeah! And what are these old books?

BOBBY: I told you. My grandma loves garage sales.

LEXI: Yes she does . . .

BOBBY: I went last weekend with her and bought these.

LEXI: Trash!

MOLLY: It's not trash. These are cool, Bobby. I like them.

GARY: You *would* like them.

MOLLY: Be quiet. *(To BOBBY.)* So is that it? What else??

BOBBY: *(Pulling a map out from a book.)* Well . . . here's what I really want to show you guys.

GARY: What is that? A map?

BOBBY: Yep. My grandma found it in these old books.

MOLLY: Cool!

LEXI: *(Pointing.)* Look where it leads to . . .

GARY: Where . . .?

BOBBY: The Jonestown Cemetery.

MOLLY: The cemetery??

GARY: *(Humorously.)* Ohhh!! The Jonestown Cemetery!

BOBBY There's a big x right here.

MOLLY: Cool. Let's go!

LEXI Not cool. I'm not going out there.

BOBBY: Neither am I. Creepy! Here, take it.
      (Passes the map to them.)

MOLLY: Well, heck. *I'll* go!

GARY: I'll go with you!

MOLLY: Good. How about tonight?

LEXI: Tonight?

MOLLY: Sure. Let's do it tonight. You guys don't wanna come?

BOBBY: Not me. All those pine trees! This is the Jonestown Cemetery. The Pine Ghost lives out there. *You* know the legend!

MOLLY: Quit. There *is* no Pine Ghost. Bobby, this is *your* map. Come on . . . it'll be fun!

BOBBY: No, keep it. That cemetery is creepy!

LEXI: Yes it is! You guys are crazy!

GARY: Molly, we can get Emma and Ava and their sisters to go with us.

MOLLY: Yeah, good idea!

BOBBY: *Those* girls . . ? Hmmmpph.

LEXI: Guys, are you sure about this??

MOLLY: Yes! There might be money there!

BOBBY: Well, *maybe* . . .

LEXI: Money?? Whatever! I doubt it!

BOBBY: There *might* be money. But I'm not going out there!

MOLLY: Dinero!

GARY: Money!

MOLLY: Cash! Dinero en el graveyard!

BOBBY: Huh . . . ?

MOLLY: Dinero en el graveyard! You know, *money in the graveyard!*

GARY: Yep!

LEXI: All right, enough of this nonsense. We have drum class. Let's go, Bobby.

>   *(They all begin to exit. BOBBY and LEXI leave together, MOLLY and GARY leave together.)*

GARY: And *we* have history. Later!

BOBBY: Have fun this weekend! In the cemetery!! With the *Pine Ghost!*

MOLLY: When we find that money, I'll accept your apology.

GARY: Hah!

BOBBY: Please! There's no money out there!

LEXI: Later, guys!

MOLLY: Bye!

(*Everybody exits. End of scene.*)

SCENE TWO

The local cemetery. Except for BOBBY and LEXI, the entire cast enters, slowly and quietly.

MIGUEL: Wow . . .

McKENNA: This is scary!

AVA: This is cool!

EMMA: Ssshh!!

MOLLY: What? Nobody's out here!

McKENNA: What about the Pine Ghost?

MIGUEL: Yeah!

GARY: Hush. There is no Pine Ghost.

McKENNA: How do you know? Look at all these pine trees!

EMMA: Oh, stop it.

MOLLY: Yeah. I thought you guys were brave.

AVA: Molly, do you have the map?

MOLLY: Right here.

EMMA: Great. Let's have a look!

McKENNA: Why is that tree branch moving?

GARY: Hush! That's the wind.

MIGUEL: Are you sure?

AVA: Yes, we're sure!!

McKENNA: Do you know why he's called the Pine Ghost?

MOLLY: Why?

MIGUEL: Because he lives in the pine trees!!

MOLLY: Guys, quit! *(Looking at the map.)* Okay . . . let's have a look. Hmmm. The X is by two graves.

EMMA: Well . . . here are the two graves.

GARY: *(Looking at map.)* And it's also by the pine trees.

AVA: Here are the pine trees.

McKENNA: Don't remind me!!

GARY: Stop! Come on! Help us look . . . *(Looking at map)*

MOLLY: It shows the X is right here . . . right by the second grave.

EMMA: Yep. *(Pointing at map.)* There it is.

MOLLY: Okay. Let's dig!

    (AVA and EMMA begin to dig.)

McKENNA: Right here?

MOLLY: Yes! X marks the spot, silly.

MIGUEL: All right! Get to it, you two! Start digging.

GARY: *(Singing)* "Money in the Graveyard . .!"

EMMA: Great. Maybe your singing will scare away the Pine Ghost.

MOLLY: There *is* no Pine Ghost. Come on. Dig!

EMMA: We are!

MIGUEL: Yeah!

McKENNA: *(Hearing something.)* Umm . . what is *that?*

AVA: *(Discovering something in the hole.)* Umm . . . what is *that?*

(Everyone except for McKENNA and MIGUEL stares down into the hole, curious. McKENNA is scared of what she heard.)

GARY: What is it . .?

McKENNA: *(Staring off into woods.)* Did you guys hear that . . ?

EMMA: A bag!

McKENNA: Ummm . . . guys?

GARY: A *what*?

EMMA: A bag! A bag of money!

AVA: Come on . . . help me grab it.

(MOLLY, AVA, and EMMA all carefully lift the bag. There are stacks of money falling out of the top of the bag.)

McKENNA: I heard something!

MIGUEL: So did I!

MOLLY: It's heavy!

McKENNA: Guys! It's the Pine Ghost!

GARY: McKenna, stop!

MIGUEL: It's true!

AVA: Look at all this money!!

McKENNA: We should go . . !

EMMA: Molly, you guys were right! It's money!

GARY: Lots of it!

AVA: We can retire!

MOLLY: What do you mean, *we*? This was our idea!!

GARY: Well, there's enough to go around! We're rich!

MOLLY: *(Grabbing the money, begins to exit.)* Come on! Let's get out of here!

AVA: Let's go!

McKENNA: This place freaks me out!

MIGUEL: You got that right!

EMMA: Oh, be quiet!

AVA: Yeah, *everything* freaks you two out!

   (They exit in a hurry. End of scene.)

SCENE THREE

Monday morning, at school. BOBBY and LEXI are standing, looking at a notebook/papers for class. Enter GARY and MOLLY, who promptly walk over to them.

GARY: Well, well, well . . . look what the cat dragged in!

BOBBY: Oh. Hi!

LEXI: Um . . buenos días!

MOLLY: Buenos días to *you!* Have a good weekend?

BOBBY: Uh . . what?

GARY: Did you guys have a good weekend?

LEXI: Yeah.

BOBBY: I guess so. How about you guys?

GARY: Oh, sure.

MOLLY: It was wonderful.

GARY: Great.

MOLLY: Fantastic.

(BOBBY and LEXI nervously attempt to leave.)

BOBBY: Okay, well, we have class now.

LEXI: Yep!

MOLLY: *(Grabs his arm.)* Not. So. Fast!

LEXI: Uh . . what's wrong?

MOLLY: What's wrong? What's wrong?? *(Pulls out a handful of fake money.)* Does *this* look familiar?

BOBBY: Oh! You found the money!

LEXI: Super!

GARY: Not super! This money is fake!

BOBBY: What?

MOLLY: And you guys know it!

GARY: Drop the act! You two buried this fake money in the graveyard!

LEXI: *(To BOBBY.)* Ughh! See?? I told you she'd be upset!

BOBBY: Oh, guys . . . we are sorry!

LEXI: So sorry!!

BOBBY: Please forgive us! We thought it would be funny!

GARY: Funny? We were in a *graveyard*!!

MOLLY: In the middle of the night!

GARY: On a wild goose chase!!

BOBBY: *(Sadly.)* I know . . . .

LEXI: *(To BOBBY.)* I told you it was a bad idea!

BOBBY: You never told me that!

LEXI: Yes I did!

MOLLY: Whatever. Okay, here is what we want . .

LEXI: What is it?

MOLLY: You two are going to carry our backpacks.

BOBBY: Your . . . backpacks?

GARY: Yes. All week. Beginning *now*!

LEXI: Now??

MOLLY: Yep.

BOBBY: Um . . . okay.

LEXI: Okay. That's only fair. I guess.

MOLLY: You can carry them from class to class. Get our backpacks, Gary.

> *(MOLLY turns to face the backpacks as GARY goes to get them. BOBBY and LEXI try to sneak away as her back is turned.)*

GARY*:* Backpacks on the way!

MOLLY: Yep! I'm going to enjoy this. *(Turns to see them running away.)* Hey! Wait a minute!!

BOBBY: Later, guys!

LEXI: Gotta go!

> *(AVA and EMMA abruptly enter, blocking their exit.)*

AVA: Excuse me . . . ?

EMMA: Going somewhere??

LEXI: Ohhh!

BOBBY: Aghhh!

> *(They run to the other side of the stage and try to exit. Enter MIGUEL and McKENNA, who abruptly block their exit.)*

MIGUEL: Hello?!?

McKENNA: Going somewhere??

BOBBY: Agghh!

LEXI: No!!

(They turn to see GARY holding out the backpacks; they face the audience and crumble to the ground as GARY drops the backpacks on top of them.)

BOBBY & LEXI: Agggghhhh!

(Lights fade. End of play.)

A Day In Court

A Day In Court

<u>Characters</u>

ONE   The judge. Serious. Stern.

TWO   The defense.

THREE   The prosecution.

FOUR   The defendant. Loves to speak español.

FIVE   Bailiff.

SIX   A newsie.

The setting is a courtroom. The case is just getting started as the play begins.

Needs: a gavel, a tall American flag. The judge wears a black robe, and SIX wears the typical clothing of a "newsie."

A courtroom. The case is just getting started as the play begins.

ONE Okay, okay . . . settle down, everybody. *(Tap-tap)* Settle down. Let's come to attention. The Morgantown District Court calls the case of Spanish 311 to the stand.

FIVE *(To TWO and FOUR)* Come forth, please. Are we ready?

FOUR Sí.

FIVE Raise your right hand.

FOUR Okay.

FIVE Do you promise to tell the whole truth?

FOUR Qué?

FIVE Do you promise to tell the whole truth??

FOUR Sí! La verdad! Always la verdad!

FIVE *(Pointing to the chair.)* Okay, please sit here.

FOUR Claro.

TWO Your honor, my client is being accused of something very, very silly.

ONE And what is that??

TWO She's accused of speaking too much Spanish!

ONE Hmmm. Too much Spanish, huh?

TWO That's right. This lawsuit is unfair!

FOUR No es justo!

TWO Ridiculous!

FOUR Ridículo!

TWO Just plain bad!

FOUR Malo!

TWO Okay, easy . . . .

ONE Well . . . *(to FOUR)* . . is this true? Do you speak too much Spanish??

FOUR Sí! A mí me gusta!

ONE What?

FOUR A mí me encanta! I love Español!

THREE I object!! This person is trying to influence you with her emotional words! She's out of line!

TWO Not true, your honor.

FOUR No es verdad!

ONE *(To THREE)* Let her finish.

THREE Uggghh.

TWO Anyway, my client is being harassed. She loves Spanish. She enjoys a foreign language! Why is that a problem?? *(Hitting table)* Why?

FOUR Por qué? Por qué??

TWO *(Calming FOUR)* Easy!

FOUR Oh . . . sorry.

ONE Well, it is true that *some* people might be bothered by hearing so much Spanish.

THREE Exactly!

ONE I mean, not *everybody* speaks the language. Right?

FOUR Pero es bonita! Una idioma de belleza! Las palabras . . .

ONE Miss?

FOUR Las frases . . .

ONE Miss?

FOUR Las expresiones!!

ONE Miss!! *(Banging the gavel.)* Order in the court!

FIVE Uh . . . does that mean it's lunchtime??

ONE No!

THREE It means to be quiet!!

ONE Um, *I'm* in charge here . . .

THREE Oh, sorry, your honor.

ONE *(To THREE)* Now, counselor . . . what is your position?

THREE Well, as you can see . . . the defendant simply speaks too much Spanish. It drives people crazy! She says *que* and not *what*. *Por favor* instead of *please*. *Él* instead of *he*. *Ella* instead of *she*.

FOUR Don't forget *uvas* instead of *grapes!*

FIVE *Uvas?? Now* is it time for lunch??

ONE Bailiff! *(Tap-tap.)* I am warning you!!

FIVE Sorry!

ONE Well . . . goodness. What we have here, folks, is one big mess. *(Looks back and forth between THREE and FOUR.)* You say hello, you say hola. You say cake, you say pastel. You say tomato-

FOUR And I say tomáto!!

FIVE Ha!

ONE Quiet!

TWO I say tomáto too!

    (Tap-tap)

THREE Well, I say tomato!!

ONE Order!

TWO Who cares what you say??

THREE What??

FOUR *(To THREE)* Yeah, who cares??

ONE *(Tap-tap)* I am warning all of you!!

THREE Bring it!!

TWO Oh, it's been *brought!!*

FOUR Ándele!!

ONE Order!! *(Tap-tap)*

(Enter SIX, carrying a newspaper, newsie-style)

THREE Your honor, they started it!!

SIX Extra, extra! Read all about it!!

ONE What is this?

SIX Everybody, guess what!!

FIVE What is it??

SIX The news just came out!! It's fine to speak Spanish whenever you want!

TWO It is . . ?

SIX Sure it is!! Look! It's in today's paper! Everybody's doing it!

FIVE Wow. The front page of the Morgantown Times! Look at that!

ONE Well, if it's good enough for them, it's good enough for me. *(To FOUR)* Miss, your case is dismissed. *(Tap.)* Congratulations!

TWO Hooray!!

THREE I don't believe it!! *(Grabs the newspaper and rips it in half. SIX groans, throws up his hands and quickly exits.)*

FOUR Spanish forever!!

FIVE Congratulations!

TWO Increíble! Òrale!

THREE I quit!

TWO You can't quit!!

THREE Yes I can. I'm going into teaching.

TWO What??

THREE You heard me! I'll see you guys in class. *(Exits.)*

FOUR Well, time to celebrate! Come on, let's go get some fried chicken!

TWO Okay! You, uh, you're gonna pay me, right? Law school wasn't cheap, you know.

FOUR We'll talk about it over dinner. *(They begin to exit.)* You take pesos, don't you??

TWO Uh, I think . . . .

FOUR And if not, I've got this big jar of pennies at home.

TWO Uh . . . okay.

FOUR I'll let you count them out for me.

(*TWO groans as she and FOUR exit.*)

ONE Well bailiff . . . that was crazy.

FIVE Sí. Oops, I mean *yes*.

ONE No, no, *sí* is fine. What time is our next case?

FIVE Judge, we're finished! That was the last case for the day!

ONE Was it?

FIVE Sí!

ONE Ahhh . . . fantástico. Well, quieres comer?

FIVE Sí. Tengo hambre.

ONE Let's go to Bobby's diner.

FIVE Sure. That place has great cake.

ONE It also has good ice cream.

FIVE You mean *helado.*

ONE Right. And you mean *pastel.*

FIVE Are we doing what I think we're doing?

ONE Yes, we are!

FIVE Órale!

(They exit, laughing. End of play.)

Mrs. Calapooza and the Culebra

Mrs. Calapooza and the Culebra

Characters

MRS. CALAPOOZA   A teacher, in her sixties or seventies. Stern, grouchy. Played by an adult or a student with a wig and proper clothing.

KATIE   A student. Aggressive. Feisty.

LUKE   A student. Kind.

ISABELLA   A student. Passive.

SIMONE   A student. Kind.

The time is the present, the place a classroom, during a Spanish quiz. The students are seated at tables or in desks, and Mrs. Calapooza is at her desk/table, going through various papers. She has a large bag or purse beside her desk. There should be some distance between her and the others.

There are Spanish words and phrases woven throughout the play but students of any race or ethnicity can perform this play.

AT RISE: A school day. All four students are in the class, furiously studying. MRS. CALAPOOZA is at her desk, looking at various papers.

KATIE: Agghh! I'm so tired of these Spanish quizzes!

ISABELLA: I know. So many words!

LUKE: Mrs. Calapooza drives me bananas.

SIMONE: Mantequilla.

LUKE: What?

SIMONE: You said 'bananas.' It's *mantequilla*, in Spanish.

KATIE: Bananas is *plátanos*, you dope.

LUKE: No, I thought bananas was *bananas*.

ISABELLA: I think it's both.

SIMONE: Oh, right. Mantequilla is *butter*. Sorry.

LUKE: Well, whatever. *(Looking back at his notes.)* Aghh! I'm not ready for this!

ISABELLA: Me neither!!

KATIE: Well, don't worry. I took care of our little situation. Ha, ha . . .

SIMONE: Really?

ISABELLA: Did you hide it??

KATIE: Yes! It's all taken care of!
       (She points in MRS. CALAPOOZA's direction.)
Right up there!

MRS. CALAPOOZA: Okay, class. *(Gets up, walks over and begins to hand out the quiz papers.)* Let's begin!

LUKE: *(To KATIE.)* I can't believe you!!

KATE: Sshhh!!

MRS. CALAPOOZA: Listos??

SIMONE: Can we have a little more time to study?

MRS. CALAPOOZA: NO! Put all papers away.

ISABELLA: Ohhh!

MRS. CALAPOOZA: Now!

LUKE: Okay! Okay!

MRS. CALAPOOZA: Let's begin. Ready? Número uno . . . pastel!

(Pause. They all fidget, trying to remember.)

MRS. CALAPOOZA: Pastel!
(Pause.)
Número dos . . . cebolla!

ISABELLA: Ohhh . . what is cebolla?

MRS. CALAPOOZA: Silencio! NO TALKING DURING THE QUIZ!!

ISABELLA: Sorry!

MRS. CALAPOOZA: Cebolla!
(Pause.)
Número tres . . . zanahoria.

KATIE: Aghh! I forgot that word!

MRS. CALAPOOZA: Sounds like a personal problem.

KATIE: Uhhhh . . .

MRS. CALAPOOZA: Zanahoria!
(Pause.)
Número cuatro . . . naranja!

SIMONE: Mrs. Calapooza, my pencil lead broke.

MRS. CALAPOOZA: Too bad! You should have come prepared!

SIMONE: But—

MRS. CALAPOOZA: Naranja!
        (Pause.)
Número cinco . . .

ISABELLA: Hang on!

MRS. CALAPOOZA: Papas!

LUKE: Uh, does that mean 'daddies'?

MRS. CALAPOOZA: It's going to mean an F if you don't be quiet!

LUKE: Oops! Sorry!

MRS. CALAPOOZA: Papas!
        (Pause.)
Okay, there's one more . . . pepino!
        (Pause. They continue to fidget and think.)
Pepino! Okay, your time is up!

KATIE: Already??

SIMONE: Is that it??

MRS. CALAPOOZA: Sí! You heard me! Pass me all the papers.

KATIE: Wow . . .

MRS. CALAPOOZA: *(As she collects them.)* Gracias . . gracias . . .

SIMONE: *(Still dazed.)* Good Lord . . .

MRS. CALAPOOZA: Gracias.

(The bell rings. They all get up slowly to exit. MRS. CALAPOOZA walks back to her desk. She eventually goes over to her bag.)

MRS. CALAPOOZA: Hasta luego, clase.

ISABELLA: Bye.

LUKE: Hasta luego.

(Pause as they all come together, depressed, to talk.)

SIMONE: Man! She is so mean!

KATIE: And did you see how fast she went on that quiz?

LUKE: I know! No time at all!

ISABELLA: It's just crazy. They should have hired somebody else for Spanish.

SIMONE: I know. Someone like that guy Mr. Glass.

ISABELLA: Yeah! He rocked.

LUKE: Guys . . . look. She's getting her bag!

ISABELLA: Is she?

KATIE: There she goes! This is it!

(MRS. CALAPOOZA opens her bag, pulls out a large rubber snake and screams, throwing it up in the air in horror. She grabs her chest and falls to the ground. The students all gasp and shriek.)

KATIE: We did it! The culebra always wins!

ISABELLA: What are you talking about it?? You may have given her a heart attack!!

(They all run over to her.)

SIMONE: Mrs. Calapooza!!

LUKE: Mrs. Calapooza!

(They lean down over her.)

ISABELLA: Mrs. Calapooza, can you hear us? Are you okay?

(Long pause. Nothing.)

KATIE: Oh, what have we done??

SIMONE: We need to give her CPR!!

KATIE: Uh . . .CPR?

(They all cringe and look at each other.)

LUKE: Uhhh . . .

ISABELLA: Uhh . . .

LUKE: Mrs. Calapooza??

SIMONE: Mrs. Calapooza . . . can you hear us??

(She quickly opens her eyes and looks right at them.)

MRS. CALAPOOZA: Of course I can hear you!
(Sitting up.)

ISABELLA: Agghh!

KATIE: Ohhh!

MRS. CALAPOOZA: What do you think I am? Deaf?
(Standing up quickly.)

LUKE: So you're . . . okay?

ISABELLA: You didn't have a heart attack?

MRS. CALAPOOZA: I was fooling the whole time!

SIMONE: Ah, man!

MRS. CALAPOOZA: That's right! I know you guys put that rubber snake in there! That *culebra*! The question is . . . *who?*

KATIE: *(Pointing at LUKE.)* He did it!

LUKE: No, she did! *(Pointing at ISABELLA.)*

ISABELLA: I didn't do it!!

MRS. CALAPOOZA: So, who's lying then? Huh? *All* of you??

KATIE: No!!

SIMONE & **LUKE:** No!!

ISABELLA: *I'm* not lying!!

MRS. CALAPOOZA: Get out of here!! All of you! You're gonna be late for class!!

    (They all run out of the class.)

MRS. CALAPOOZA: Go!! And don't you ever try a trick like that again!! Do you hear me? EVER!!

(Pause. She picks up the snake and plays with it. She faces the audience, lightly laughing, in an evil-like manner.)

MRS. CALAPOOZA: Culebra, culebra, my little culebra . . . don't these kiddies know? Teachers always know. Yes, that's right. We always know!

(She smiles at the snake as she sits down and begins to grade papers. End of play.)

Don't Let Bigfoot Bite!

Don't Let Bigfoot Bite!

ALAINA	Camper. Scared of Bigfoot.
TEDDY	Camper. Scared of Bigfoot.
AVA	Camper. Scared of Bigfoot.
ISABELLA	Camper. Does not believe in Bigfoot.
KEN	Camper. Does not believe in Bigfoot.
VALENTINA	Park Ranger.
DYLAN	Park Ranger.

The campers are camping out in a state park and are about to go to bed. The park rangers are talking to them. There are sleeping bags on the ground, pillows, etc. A small fire is nearby.

Needs: a small campfire, a large set of dried foot-prints, flashlights, sleeping bags, pajamas, park ranger shirts/badges/hats, cell phone, pine straw, pinecones, twigs, etc. The sound effect of a large animal or "monster" in the woods is needed.

As the lights go up, a loud, eerie noise is heard from the forest.

ALAINA: See? Don't you hear that?

VALENTINA: It's a wolf.

ALAINA: It's not a wolf! Wolves don't sound like that!!

AVA: Right!

VALENTINA: Look, calm down. Okay? There's no Bigfoot in these woods. That sound was a wolf.

TEDDY: Hmmmph.

DYLAN: Guys, Bigfoot doesn't exist.

VALENTINA: It's probably your friend out there, in the other campground.

ISABELLA: That's what I told them!

TEDDY: *(Holding up a dried, muddy footprint.)* Then how do you explain this footprint??

VALENTINA: Anybody could do that!

ISABELLA: Anybody!!

TEDDY: Are you sure?? Look how big this thing is!

VALENTINA: Yes, I'm sure! This was just a trick!

DYLAN: Your friend probably did that. With some big wooden feet. Where is your friend, anyway?

AVA: *(Pointing off to the woods.)* Over there. In campground number 4.

TEDDY: *(To the rangers.)* Yeah, his name is Jimmy. His family didn't want to camp with us.

DYLAN: Oh. Okay.

AVA: Yeah, they're kind of weird.

VALENTINA: Well . . . . Jimmy's probably the one that's doing it. That's all.
  (Begins to leave.)
And look, we have to go. We have to go check on a pack of wild raccoons in campsite number one.

ALAINA: Okay . . .

VALENTINA: Remember, guys . . . . that sound was a wolf.

AVA: If you say so . . .

DYLAN: There *is* no Bigfoot. We promise.

VALENTINA: You guys get some sleep, okay? It's late. We need to go.

DYLAN: Yeah, these raccoons are waiting for us.

VALENTINA: Good night.

TEDDY: Bye.

ISABELLA: Bye.

KEN: Later.

(VALENTINA and DYLAN exit.)

ISABELLA: See? I told you there was no Bigfoot out here!

KEN: Yeah, it's just Jimmy and his family, playing a joke. You know how Jimmy is.

ALAINA: But I don't know . . . how would he make that sound?

ISABELLA: Who knows? Maybe his dad has a horn or something.

KEN: His dad has all kinds of weird things in his garage.

ALAINA: Whatever.

AVA: Well . . . come on, we had a long day. It's bed-time.

(They begin to turn in.)

TEDDY: I am beat!

KEN: Me too.

ALAINA: But what about Bigfoot??

ISABELLA: There is no Bigfoot! He doesn't exist!

AVA: I'm not so sure . . . !

ALAINA: Ohhhh . . .!

ISABELLA: Come on, guys. It's bedtime.

KEN: Yeah, I'm tired. We can talk about large, hairy creatures that *don't exist* in the morning.

ALAINA: *(Sighing.)* Good night . . .

AVA: Good night.

TEDDY: Night night . . sleep tight . . .

ISABELLA & KEN: Don't let Bigfoot bite!

ALAINA: Don't do that!!

ISABELLA: *(Evil cackle.)* Ha ha . . . sorry!

> *(They close their eyes and try to go to sleep. Long pause. An owl is heard.)*

ALAINA: What is that??

ISABELLA: What??

ALAINA: That sound!!

KEN: An owl.

ALAINA: What?

ISABELLA: It's an owl!

KEN: Yeah. Don't you know what an owl sounds like??

ALAINA: Ohhh . . !

(Pause. The hooting is heard again.)

ALAINA: There is it again!!

KEN: It's an owl!!

ALAINA: Are you sure??

ISABELLA: Go to sleep, Alaina!!

KEN: Yeah!!

ALAINA: Ohhh!!!

(Long pause. The eerie noise is heard from the woods again.)

ALAINA: What is that??

ISABELLA: Probably a small animal. A rabbit. Maybe a squirrel.

ALAINA: How do you know??

KEN: Go to sleep! Good grief!!

ALAINA: TEDDY!! AVA! Aren't you guys scared too? *(Pause.)* Guys???

ISABELLA: They're sleeping.

KEN: They're sound asleep. You should be asleep too.

ALAINA: Ohhhh! Whatever.

ISABELLA: I knew we shouldn't have brought you camping.

ALAINA: Huh??

KEN: It's true! You are ruining the whole trip!

ISABELLA: It's true!! Now go to sleep!

> *(Long pause. The eerie noise in the woods is heard again.)*

ALAINA: There it is!!

KEN: It's just a squirrel or something! We told you. *(Beat.)* Why did you come camping with us??

ISABELLA: Yeah, why??

ALAINA: Sorry.

ISABELLA: You are scared of everything!!

KEN: Yep.

ISABELLA: And you are ruining our camping trip!! *(Pause.)* Now, please . . . . can we go to sleep?

ALAINA: Yes.

ISABELLA: Thank you!!

(Long pause. ALAINA feels bad.)

ALAINA: Guys . . ? Um, still awake?

KEN: Yes!!

ISABELLA: What is it, Alaina??

ALAINA: Guys, I'm sorry. Please forgive me. Oh, please forgive me! It's true, I *am* scared of everything. I came on this trip to get over being scared. And . . . well . . . I'm not doing a great job.

KEN: It's okay.

ISABELLA: Yeah. You'll get there. I know it's hard. I used to be scared of the woods all the time. But now I love it out here.

ALAINA: I know you do.

ISABELLA: You'll get there.

KEN: Yeah.

ALAINA: Well, thanks a lot. That means a lot to me. I know there's no Bigfoot out there . . . but I just get scared sometimes.

KEN: It's okay.

ISABELLA: It's fine.

ALAINA: Well, I appreciate it. *(Pause.)* Okay! Now I feel better. Good night!

KEN: Good night.

ISABELLA: 'Night.

(Long pause. The eerie noise is heard again.)

ALAINA: Um . . . . it's just an owl, right?

KEN: Yep. Just an owl or something.

(The eerie noise is heard again.)

ALAINA: *(Becoming more scared.)* Yep. Only an owl.

ISABELLA: That's right. *(Beat. Sits up and looks at her cell phone.)* Oh, what is this? My phone . . .

KEN: Huh?

ISABELLA: I got a text.

KEN: What?? You brought your phone out here??

ISABELLA: Yes.

KEN: Brother . . .

ISABELLA: My parents made me. In case I had to call them. *(Reading the text.)* Um . . . guys?

ALAINA: What?

ISABELLA: It's from Jimmy's mom.

KEN: Well . . . ? What does she say?

TEDDY: *(Waking up, yawning.)* Are you guys *ever* going to sleep??

AVA: *(Also waking up.)* Yeah!!

TEDDY: Man!

ISABELLA: *(Still reading.)* Oh no!

ALAINA: What?

ISABELLA: She says that they left!!

AVA: What??

ISABELLA: Jimmy's family left the campsite! His dad got sick and they had to leave!! They left an hour ago!!

KEN: Oh. So . . . if they left . . then who is making those noises??

ISABELLA: Um . . .

TEDDY: Um . . .

ALAINA: Um . . .

EVERYBODY: BIGFOOT!

(They all scramble to get up.)

ISABELLA: Let's go!

ALAINA: Come on!

AVA: Let's get outta here!!

ALAINA: I *told* you guys!!

ISABELLA: Oh, be quiet!

ALAINA: I did tell you!

TEDDY: No, *we* told them!

ALAINA: I want an apology!!

> *(Enter DYLAN and VALENTINA, terrified, out of breath.)*

KEN: And *I* want to live! Come on!

ISABELLA: Run!

DYLAN: Hey campers!

KEN: What??

VALENTINA: Guess who we just saw??

ALAINA: We're way ahead of you!

> *(The eerie noise is heard again.)*

EVERYBODY: Agghhhhh!!!

> *(They all exit in a scramble, screaming, running, etc. End of play.)*

The Great Galapanza

The Great Galapanza
Characters

ONE   Weary of Galapanza.

TWO   Weary of Galapanza.

THREE   Is very patient with Galapanza.

FOUR   Bella. "Disappears" in the magic box.

FIVE   Galapanza the Magician. Very
               cocky. Conceited.

SIX   Weary of Galapanza.

SEVEN   Weary of Galapanza.

EIGHT   Weary of Galapanza.

Galapanza is getting ready for a big magic show and she needs to practice in front of her friends. But she is full of herself! She brags and is very conceited. The others teach her a lesson.

Needs: Galapanza wears the traditional clothing of a magician. She will need two or three basic magic tricks. Cards, hat, toy rabbit, etc. A giant cardboard box. A large <u>wardrobe box</u> works perfectly, usually obtainable at a moving/storage business.

124

As the play opens, everyone is waiting for Galapanza. She is arriving to practice for her show. Everyone is generally weary of her attitude.

ONE Ughhh. Where is she?

TWO I know. I just wanna go home.

FOUR Me too.

THREE Come on, it'll be fine. She just wants to practice.

SIX She *always* wants to practice.

THREE It won't take long.

ONE Neither does a root canal!

TWO Ha!

FOUR She drives me crazy.

SIX And she's so bossy!

TWO I know. *Bossy* isn't the word.

ONE *(Sarcastically.)* Hocus-pocus . . . abracadabra . . .

FOUR Here she comes!

TWO Oh, I can't wait!

ONE I know . . .

(Enter FIVE)

FIVE Hey there! Okay, so are we all set?

SIX Yeah . . . I guess . .

ONE Do we really have to do this?

TWO Yeah! Do we??

FIVE Please! I just want to practice for my magic show. That's all!

FOUR Ugghh!

THREE Come on, guys. It won't take long.

(They all begin to sit down)

FIVE I just want to practice! My show is next Saturday.

SIX We know, we know . . .

FOUR Personally, I'm tired of magic.

ONE I'm tired of *her* magic.

TWO No kidding.

FIVE Okay . . . all set? Ready?

THREE Sure. Let's do it.

FIVE Okay, the great Galapanza is here. To show you her magic!
(Pause as she prepares her trick)
Okay. Um. Bazito, bazita . . .

SIX Huh??

FIVE Silence, child!

SIX Oops!

FIVE I need to concentrate!

SIX Sorry!

TWO Yeah, let her *concentrate.*

FIVE Okay. Wazito, wazita . . . hocos, pocus . . .
(Does the trick)
Tah-dah!!
(Pause. She looks at them)
What? No applause??

THREE Oh, right!

(They begin to applaud, slowly.)

ONE Sorry!

FOUR Ughh. Sheesh.

FIVE Thank you, thank you . . .

TWO *(Sarcastically.)* You're welcome.

SIX Good grief.

FIVE That's more like it! And now . . . on to my next trick . . .
        (Begins to do the new trick.)
 Okay. Ready? Bazito, bazita . . . abracadabra . .
        (Does the trick)
Tah-dah!!

THREE Cool.

FIVE Of course it's cool!

THREE Um. Okay.

FIVE It's magnificent!

FOUR Right.

TWO Magnificent . . .

FIVE All my tricks are *magnificent!*

ONE Hmmpph.

SIX If you say so.

FIVE And now, for the grand finale! Bella?

FOUR Yes?

FIVE All set? Are you ready?

FOUR Sure. I'm ready.

FIVE Okay. In the box you go.

FOUR Okay! *(She does so.)*

FIVE Right this way. There we go. Thank you, thank you . . .

FOUR You're welcome.

FIVE We'll close the door. Okay. Just like that. *(Pause. She is preparing the trick.)* Okay. Here we go. Wazito, wazita . . . hoco poco . .

FOUR *(Opening the door.)* Don't you mean hocus-pocus?

FIVE Silence child!

FOUR Sorry!

FIVE Get back in there! I must concentrate!

ONE *(Sarcastically.)* Yeah, she's gotta concentrate.

TWO Give me a break . . .

FIVE Okay . . . let's try it again. Bazito, bazita . . . wazito, wazita . . . tah-dah!!
        (Opens the door. Bella is gone. Nobody claps.)
What?? No applause??

SIX Oh, right!

        (They begin to clap.)

ONE Sorry! We forgot!

TWO Good job!

ONE Mehhhh . . .

SIX Even though we've seen this trick a million times.

FIVE Thank you, thank you! And now . . . I'll bring the disappearing lady back!

ONE Don't you mean *Bella*??

FIVE Silence, child!

ONE Oops!

FIVE I must concentrate!

TWO Yeah. Don't you know she's gotta concentrate??

FIVE Okay. Here we go . . . Abraca-dos . . . abraca-tres . . . tah-dah!!
> *(She opens the door. Nobody is there. Closes the door and tries again.)*

I said, "tah-dah!!"
> *(Nothing happens).*

Um. What happened?

ONE Where is she??

FIVE Hold on, everybody! Let me try it again.
> *(Looking back at the box. Closes the door, opens it again.)*

I said, "TAH-DAH!!"
> *(Nothing happens)*

TWO Bella?

THREE Where is she?

FIVE Where'd she go?

> *(They all begin to look.)*

ONE Bella!!

FIVE I don't believe this!

SIX She's actually gone! Nobody's back here!

THREE Bella!!

ONE You actually made her . . disappear?? How could you?

TWO Bring her back!! Now!

FIVE I don't know how! *(Pulls off hat, looks at it)*

THREE You don't know how??

FIVE No! I mean, my grandfather always told me this hat had special powers. But . . .

SIX Come on, guys.

THREE To where?

ONE We've gotta tell Bella's parents! This is serious!

   (They begin to gradually exit.)

TWO But she has to be here somewhere!!

ONE Where??

THREE Yeah, we looked all over that box. She's not here.

SIX Maybe she *is* a real magician!

TWO Yeah, an evil magician!

THREE Yeah!

FIVE Wait!

TWO We're outta here.

ONE Later, Galapanza!

FIVE Come back! Help me find her!! Come back!!

> *(They exit. She sits down, stares at the box in confusion.)*

FIVE Ohhhhh! What am I gonna do . . ? What am I gonna do . . ?

> *(Lights fade to black. Brief music interlude. Lights back up. Galapanaza and THREE are sitting down. Galapanza is very depressed.)*

FIVE My life is over. Ughhhh. This can't be happening.

THREE It's okay. It's okay . . .

FIVE No! It's *not* okay. Bella is gone! Gone!

THREE Well . . .

FIVE And it's all my fault! This hat really is magical! Ughhh!

THREE She'll come back . . . I hope.

FIVE Ohhhh!! My life is ruined. I'm gonna go to prison.

THREE No, you're not.

(Enter ONE, TWO, SIX, SEVEN and EIGHT.)

FIVE And eat cold rice and drink tap water every day. Just like they do in Arkansas!

THREE Oh, come on . . .

ONE *There* you guys are!!

THREE Hi.

TWO We were looking for you two.

FIVE Um. *(To SEVEN and EIGHT)* You guys . . . heard what happened?

SEVEN Yes.

EIGHT And we can't believe it.

SEVEN How could you??

FIVE Ohhhh, stop! I know what I did!

EIGHT Shame, shame . . .

ONE Come on, Galapanza. You have to practice!

SIX Yeah, come on. Your magic show is next week.

FIVE I don't want to.

TWO Come on. Practice . . . *(Nudging her to stand up.)*

SEVEN Yeah, let's go.

FIVE Ugghhh.

SIX Here is your wand. *(Passes it to her.)*

FIVE Ugghh, I'm not in the mood!

THREE Come on! The great Galapanza must practice!

ONE Oh, wait! Katie, did you bring the surprise?

EIGHT Yep. Right here! *(Pulls out the blindfold)*

ONE Good! Okay, ready?

SIX All set?

FIVE For . . . ?

EIGHT Here. Put this on. *(Begins to put it on her.)*

FIVE Why?

ONE Just do it!

SEVEN It's a new trick you can use!

FIVE What?

EIGHT Just do it! Trust us!

SIX Yeah. It's a cool new trick.

FIVE Okay . . okay.

TWO You'll love it. Honestly!

EIGHT Okay. Let's see. That should be tight enough.

THREE Now . . . we have a really cool surprise to show you. Ready??

FIVE Sure. I guess so.

THREE Okay. Here we go. Uno . .
	(Out comes Bella.)
dos . . . tres!!

	(Pulls the blindfold off. GALAPANZA sees BELLA.)

FOUR Surprise!!

FIVE Bella!

FOUR Hello!

FIVE What . . . what happened? Where were you?

136

TWO What happened is that we *tricked* you!

FIVE What??

SIX That's right. We tricked you!

ONE We hid Bella!

FIVE How? Where?

FOUR Right behind that other little wall. In the box.

FIVE What? You mean there are two walls in there??

FOUR Yep. We made an extra one and we didn't tell you. A few days ago.

SEVEN She hid right behind it.

FOUR Ta-dah! I was in there the whole time.

FIVE So . . . you never were missing . . ?

FOUR No!

FIVE But why?? Why did ya'll do this?

ONE Because you were being mean!!

EIGHT Yep. You were bossy!

TWO A show-off! We wanted to teach you a lesson.

FIVE Dang . . .

SIX A *big* lesson.

FIVE Wow . . . so, Bella was okay the whole time.

FOUR Yep.

FIVE Well.
    (Pause.)
Gosh, everyone. I'm so sorry. I guess I have been kind of a jerk. Ughhh. I'm sorry.

SEVEN Well. It's true. We all want to help you with your magic. But you haven't been nice.

FIVE I know. I apologize. Seriously . . . I'll stop being so bossy.

EIGHT You promise?

FIVE I do. Honestly.

THREE Are you sure?

FIVE Yes. I promise. I want to be nicer. I really do.

ONE Well . . . what do you guys think? Can we give her a second chance?

TWO Yeah.

FOUR Yeah, I think so.

SIX Sure.

SEVEN Just don't do it again!

EIGHT Right.

FIVE Okay. I won't. I feel so bad.

FOUR Besides, what you do is only *magic.*

THREE Right. It's not like it's real or anything.

FIVE What??

ONE Yeah. It's all make-believe.

FIVE Now, wait just a minute!!

TWO It's true!

FIVE Don't be so sure of that!

SIX It's true, Galapanza. Your magic isn't real.

FIVE If it's not real . . . then where are your cell phones?

SEVEN Huh?

FIVE Go ahead. Try to call somebody.

(They all reach for their phones.)

THREE Mine's right here.

ONE Yep. Me too.

THREE Wait. It *was* here!

ONE Huh?? Where the heck is it?? Did you . . ?

FIVE *(Pulling her cape back, showing their phones taped/attached to the inside of the cape.)* Looking for these??

EVERYBODY Gaspppppp!!

FOUR How did she get those??

THREE How??

TWO Maybe . . . maybe her magic is real!

ONE Maybe she's an evil wizard!!

SIX Yeah!! Guys, run!

SEVEN Vámonos!

EIGHT Go!!

FOUR It's time for Spanish class, anyway.

EIGHT Run!!

EVERYBODY Aghhhhhhh!!!!

(They all exit. GALAPANZA cackles and watches them run.)

FIVE Ha ha. That's right!! Run! Run away, you scoundrels!! Run!! And never forget . . . I am the great Galapanza!! Always . . . and forever!!

(End of play.)

☞ More from Student Plays ☜

Othello's Just Another Fellow

Dramedy. **Grades 5-7.** 25-35 minutes. 8 actors: 4 males, 3 females, one teacher (or student portraying a teacher) 3 to 5 extras, if needed. ****A Latino-themed play****

A group of students are involved in a school production of *Othello*, but one of them is disturbed about the lack of diversity in the play. He takes certain steps to disrupt the play but in the end is encouraged by the others to try and make a difference in another, more constructive way. A lesson is learned, and the production is saved from disaster!

Pagasqueeny's Pantry

Comedy. **Middle/High School.** 15-20 minutes. 6 actors: 3 females, 2 males. One student (or a teacher) plays the comical role of the elderly Mr. Pagasqueeny.

Three friends sneak into Mr. Pagasqueeny's home to get something that one of them left behind. But in walks Pagasqueeny and they must hide in the pantry! In this comical play, a lesson is learned about honesty and trust, but it takes a heated discussion in the pantry and a subsequent attempt to escape to find this out!

Una Carta de Abuelo

Dramedy. **Middle/High School.** 35-45 minutes. 10 actors: 1 teacher, 5 females, 4 males. (With the option of 4-5 extra actors in two scenes.)   **A Latino-themed play****

Two Latino cousins discover an old letter in their late grandfather's comic collection that they think leads to treasure! The cousins often butt heads, with one believing that he is more "Mexican," the other believing that some people make too much of a fuss about "being Mexican." Thus, they form their *own* groups in search of what Grandpa hid long ago. But what they find is actually worth more than merely silver or gold.

Barbecue at the Prom!

Dramedy. **Grades 5-8.** 25-35 minutes. 6 actors: 3 females, 3 males

It's a classic tale of guys versus girls! It's a prom committee, and everybody is supposed to work together but differences and opinions get in the way, causing the guys and girls to form their groups. For the end-of-the-year prom, one side wants pasta and lace, the other wants sports and barbecue! The two groups square off but eventually work together, demonstrating the importance of cooperation and compromise.

Going to Guatemala

Dramedy. **High School.** 50-60 minutes. 11 actors. 6 males, 5 females.   ****A Latino-themed play****

A Latino student is chosen at the last minute to join a humanitarian group from his school that is headed to Guatemala. But since his Spanish is weak, he faces ridicule and criticism from certain peers. Jealousy and anger trickle throughout the campus as the trip approaches, and the social buzz of the high school becomes even more hectic when the student's trip money is stolen on campus, jeopardizing his trip.

Stravinsky's Kitchen

Comedy. **High School/College.** 12-15 minutes. 3 actors: 3 males (or females).

Two friends secretly enter the home of an employer to obtain a forgotten object but the homeowner abruptly arrives home while they are there. As they hide in the kitchen's pantry and plot their getaway, the two talk and eventually argue, exposing the true colors of one of them. Upon their hasty exit a mistake is made, and one of them capitalizes on this mistake, resulting in his/her fortune.

Forty Whacks

Drama. Spooky. **High School/College.** 25-35 minutes. 3 actors: 2 females, 1 male.

A pair of siblings have inherited the Lizzie Borden Bed and Breakfast in New England. Although the business was run for decades in a quiet, respectable fashion, one of the siblings is over-ambitious, wanting to unearth an alleged piece of buried evidence within the house. This brings about a chilly tension between brother and sister, and perhaps within the house itself.

John Calhoun and a Thief

Drama. **College.** 35-40 minutes. 3 actors: 2 females, 1 male.

Kicked out of a university PhD program, a bitter and dejected female lifts from the library archives original copies of John Calhoun's personal documents. Counseled and consoled by her roommates, her conscience slowly gets to her; but as she seeks entry to other universities her luck turns to worse, and the subsequent decisions she makes regarding the historic papers cause this one-act play to become darker, if not funnier.

Honoring the Hijacker

Drama. **College.** 12-15 minutes. 4 actors: 2 females, 2 males.

It's 1981, the ten-year anniversary of the famed hijacker D.B. Cooper. The play's four characters are attending a "D.B. Festival" and have stayed up very late, outlasting everybody else. The late night chit-chat goes from pranks and jokes to outright volatility, and suddenly this get-together becomes something that three of the four characters didn't bargain for.

It's a Super Day at Sammy's!

Comedy. **Middle or High School.** 35-40 minutes. 9 actors: 5 females, 4 males (4 possible adults).

Jodi has found a summer job at a travel agency. But her three younger siblings can't seem to live without her! They call her at the office incessantly, which interferes with the work. The standard telephone greeting "It's a super day at Sammy's!" becomes a repeated theme of this comedy, as Jodi struggles to reach a balance between her job and her nagging siblings

Three Creepy Plays

Drama. **Middle School through College.** Three short 'creepy' plays.

Hockey Masks in Hueytown

Drama. Spooky. **High School/College.** 20-25 minutes. 4 actors: 2 males, 2 females.

Driving home for Thanksgiving break, four college students stop off in a small rural town to retrieve one of the student's old family pictures. They reluctantly enter the empty home of his deceased uncle, a former producer for the Friday the 13th movies. Strange objects are found during their search . . but when a hockey mask surfaces, everything really goes sideways.